First published in the United States of America
in 2019 by Chronicle Books LLC.

Originally published in Japan in 2017 under the title
Tsumannai Tsumannai by HAKUSENSHA.

Copyright © Shinsuke Yoshitake 2017.
English translation copyright © 2019 by Chronicle Books LLC.

Library of Congress Cataloging-in-Publication Data:
Names: Yoshitake, Shinsuke, 1973- author, illustrator.
Title: The boring book / Shinsuke Yoshitake.
Other titles: Tsumannai tsumannai. English
Description: San Francisco, California : Chronicle Books LLC, 2019. |
"Originally published in Japan in 2017 under the title Tsumannai Tsumannai
by HAKUSENSHA." | Summary: A child, bored by his toys, contemplates the
emotion and concept of boredom, and whether or not it is boring to be an
adult—or a child. Identifiers: LCCN 2018037897 | ISBN 9781452174563 (alk. paper)
Subjects: LCSH: Boredom—Juvenile fiction. | Emotions—Juvenile fiction. |
CYAC: Boredom—Fiction. | LCGFT: Picture books.
Classification: LCC PZ7.Y82552 Bo 2019 | DDC [E]—dc23 LC record
available at https://lccn.loc.gov/2018037897

Manufactured in China.

10 9 8 7 6 5 4 3 2 1

Chronicle Books LLC
680 Second Street
San Francisco, California 94107

Chronicle Books—we see things differently.
Become part of our community at www.chroniclekids.com.

THE
BORING
BOOK

Shinsuke Yoshitake

chronicle books · san francisco

Hmph.

SO BORING!

. . . . .

Wait—what makes
things boring?

Why am I bored?

What does "boring"
mean, anyway?

What if I were stuffed
into a big donut?

That sounds like fun . . .

but after being in there
for a while . . .

I'd probably be bored.

Um, how much longer
will I be in here?

Maybe it's boring to stay in the same place.

I'll try it!

So, what if I constantly changed how I sit?

Rustle

Rustle

Hey, this is kind of fun!

Rustle

Maybe it's fun
to be unique.

The more different,
the more fun!

A park like this looks fun.

But a park like this is boring.

Maybe it's fun
when things are crowded.

Maybe it's boring when things don't go as planned.

I wonder if a pill bug ever thinks, *I'm bored.*

How about a vending machine?

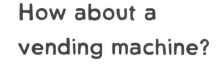

Or a rock on the street?

Or my teddy bear?

What about a straw wrapper?

Or an air conditioner?

I wonder what the world's most boring amusement park is like.

The Ferris wheel is low.

The roller coaster is slow.

Most of the rides are closed for repairs.

No way!
That would be awful!

I'd *never* go to an
amusement park
like that!

But, wait!
How strange . . .

it's actually fun to think
about "boring" things.

I mean, they're boring,
but they're also fun.

Weird!

Can everything in the world be divided into "fun" and "boring"?

Sometimes, I'm not bored *or* having fun. I'm actually not thinking about anything at all.

Like when I'm changing my clothes,

or when I'm in the bathroom,

or when I'm waiting for the light to change.

or when I'm brushing my teeth,

I wouldn't say that doing those things is fun, but it isn't boring, either. I wonder if there's a word for that experience.

Like when I'm peeling a hard-boiled egg,

or when I wake up earlier than usual,

or when I'm riding the bus.

Who came up with the word "boring" anyway?

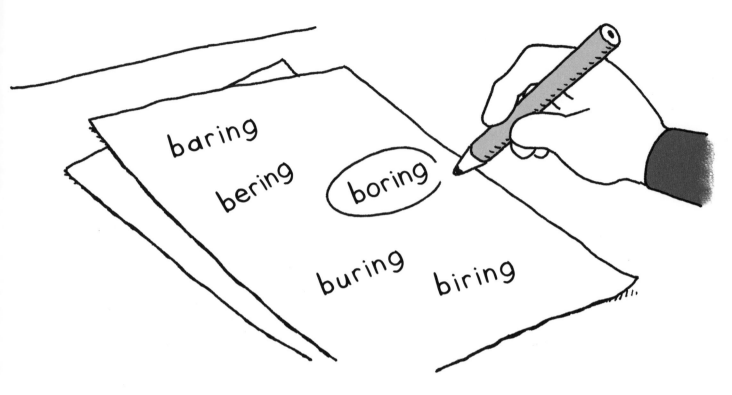

Was that person bored?

I wonder what the most boring age in a person's life is.

Grandpa, what was
the most boring thing
that ever happened
to you?

Hmmm . . .

Grandpa was
having a lot of
fun talking about
his "past boring
experiences."

Maybe boring
things turn into
fun things after
a while.

I wonder if some people look like they're having fun, but they're actually bored.

 But no matter how bored you are, it's up to you to make things fun.

There's nothing happening here . . .

so I drew a maze!

Or if some people look bored, but they're actually having fun.

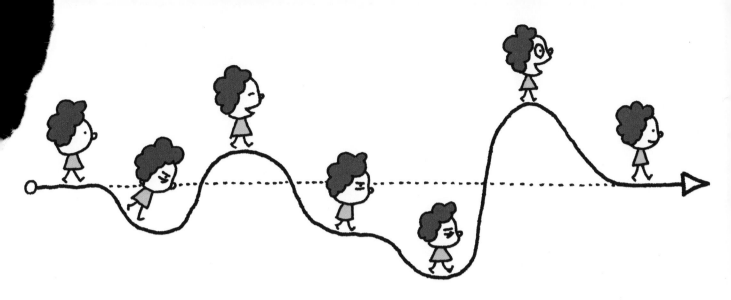

And because you get bored sometimes,
the fun experiences are even more exciting, right?